TOO
LOUD
LILY

To Gail – S. L.

ISBN 0-439-67877-3

Text copyright © 2002 by Sofie Laguna.
Illustrations copyright © 2002 by Kerry Argent. All rights reserved.
Published by Scholastic Inc. SCHOLASTIC and associated logos are
trademarks and/or registered trademarks of Scholastic Inc.

12 11 10 9 8   8 9/0

Printed in the U.S.A.   40

First Scholastic paperback printing, September 2004

The display text was set in Coop Black.
The text type was set in L VAG Rounded Light.
Book design by Yvette Awad

BY
SOFIE
LAGUNA

ILLUSTRATED
BY
KERRY
ARGENT

TOO LOUD LILY

SCHOLASTIC INC.

New York Toronto London Auckland Sydney
Mexico City New Delhi Hong Kong Buenos Aires

Everyone told Lily Hippo she was too loud.

"Lily Hippo, keep it down please – I can't hear myself think!" said Dad.

"Lily Hippo, sing quietly – you'll wake the baby!" said Mom.

"Lily Hippo, you make more noise than a herd of wild elephants!" said Lily's big brother.

Lily tried doing something very quiet. . . .

"LILY HIPPO,

NOT SO LOUD!"

they all said.

At school, Lily's best friends were Hester and Lou.

Sometimes even Hester and Lou
were upset with Lily.

She was too loud.

Then a new teacher came to Lily's school.
Her name was Miss Loopiola, and she wore
a big red poncho. She taught music and drama.

Lily liked Miss Loopiola. She decided to be in the
school play.

On the first day of rehearsals, Miss Loopiola taught everyone a fast-stomping dance.

Lily tried to do the dance very quietly.

"Wonderful work!" called out Miss Loopiola.
"But you could try stomping just a little louder
this time, please!"

Lily really liked Miss Loopiola.

Lily stomped a lot louder.

"Magnificent!" cried Miss Loopiola.

"Lily Hippo, would you like to lead the dance?"

Lily loved Miss Loopiola.

Lily was in charge of crashing the cymbals and banging the drums for storm noises, . . .

growling and roaring for the fierce lion noises, . . .

cackling and screeching for the wicked witch noises, . . .

singing the song about the very brave prince, . . .

and clapping in time to
all the music.

On the night of the play, Lily was very nervous.

What if she forgot what to do?

What if she tried to speak and no words came out?

Or even worse – what if she was too loud?

Lily could feel her heart thumping and her
knees shaking.

The room was very, very quiet.

Everybody was waiting for Lily.

"Go on Lily," whispered Miss Loopiola.

"Nice and LOUD!"

Lily took a deep breath.
"Let the show begin!"
she said in her loudest stage voice.

Lily did her best fast-stomping, . . .

her best crashing and banging, . . .

her best growling and roaring, . . .

her best cackling and screeching, . . .

and her best singing and clapping.